ISBN 9781990500084

ALL RIGHTS RESERVED

Fleshing It Out, Copyright © 2022 Karla Doyle

Editor: Grace Bradley Editing

Cover design by LoveTheCover.com

First print book publication March 2022

With the exception of quotes used in reviews, this book may not be reproduced or used in whole or in part by any means existing without written permission from the publisher, Karla Doyle.

The unauthorized reproduction or distribution of this copyrighted work is illegal. No part of this book may be scanned, uploaded or distributed via the Internet or any other means, electronic or print, without the publisher's permission. Criminal copyright infringement, including infringement without monetary gain, is punishable by law.

This book is a work of fiction and any resemblance to persons, living or dead, is purely coincidental. The characters are productions of the author's imagination. Locales are fictitious, and/or, are used fictitiously.

The publisher and author acknowledge the trademark status and trademark ownership of all trademarks, service marks and word marks mentioned in this book.

The publisher does not have any control over, and does not assume any responsibility for, third-party websites or their content.

For questions and comments about this book, please contact the author at karla@karladoyle.com.

A HOPE HARBOR ROMANCE

# KARLA DOYLE

# fleshing it out

*an older woman/younger man instalove romance*

## laura

When my son asks if I'll rent the spare bedroom to his new friend from work, I figure, why not? The house is too quiet since my twenty-five-year-old baby moved out. I never thought I'd miss the sounds of video games, but apparently, I do.

But that's not the background noise I get when Hudson moves in. Turns out, my son's coworker isn't a likeminded gaming geek. Hudson doesn't play video games. He works out. A lot.

Now my house is filled with the masculine grunting of a very fit, very handsome, younger man who owns shirts, but isn't inclined to wear them. Ditto for pants. Everywhere I turn in my tiny house, Hudson is there. Flexing. Smoldering.

I can't resist looking at him. Or using him for inspiration while I write my current romance novel. Fantasizing about him when I'm lying in my bed.

He's my tenant. My son's coworker. A man fifteen years younger than me. Hudson is fodder for my mind, but that's all he can be…until the night he puts every fantasy I've had to shame.

## hudson

House hunting is a slow process, and hotel living sucks, so I jump at the opportunity to temporarily rent a room from my coworker's mother. I'm told the place is clean, and the woman is easy to get along with. Perfect.

What the guy across the office doesn't tell me? That his

mom is ten-out-of-ten hot. Single. And sexual, if the sounds seeping through the paper-thin wall separating our bedrooms are any indication.

I'm not a pushy guy, but a man has his limits. Being perpetually hard around her, hearing her moan every night—it's more than I can take. So I make a move. A big one. And it pays off, in the best ways possible.

Our chemistry is red hot. We connect outside the bedroom, too. I'm only supposed to be here temporarily, but every minute I spend with Laura makes me determined never to leave.

# chapter one

. . .

## laura

EMPTY NESTER.

I'm an independent woman who used to laugh at the term. I never rushed my son to move out, but I always thought that once he did, I'd relish my new level of freedom. I imagined bringing a man home and having uninhibited sex. Walking around naked whenever I pleased, simply because I could.

Seth moved to his first apartment two months ago. Not only has there been no uninhibited sex in my house, I haven't had any. Zero. And I've yet to so much as streak from the bathroom to my bedroom. I can't do it, I always cover up. Old habits are hard to break.

The most exciting change to my lifestyle has been leftovers. Seth used to take them for his lunch, and now I get to eat them for mine. Who needs uninhibited sex when you have dinner leftovers for lunch? Not me, apparently.

Silence has been the hardest adjustment to living alone. I never thought I'd miss the sound of video games, but it seems I do. That's why I spent three days cleaning and painting

Seth's old bedroom, and why I'm currently focused on the street instead of my laptop.

I'm about to become a landlady. Not something I pictured myself doing, but Seth's new coworker needs a short-term rental until he finds a house to buy, and I didn't have a good reason to decline. Honestly, I'm looking forward to having noise in the house again. Being an empty nester is harder than I expected.

My pulse picks up when a sporty black coupe turns the corner. The lack of traffic on my street was part of its appeal when I bought the house after my divorce. With few exceptions, if you're on this street, it's your destination. This car is no different, its low-speed progress ending in front of my house.

I close the laptop, then stand and lean on the porch railing. My welcoming, motherly smile is in place. Waiting for the driver's door to open, I draw a breath and prepare to greet my new tenant…until he steps out.

My son is an adorable geek. Gangly, still growing into manhood, even at twenty-five. I've met his other coworkers, all of whom fall into adjacent geeky categories. Not the one looking at me over the hood of his car though. Oh no. This man is exactly that—a man. Tall, dark, and handsome as they come.

"You must be Laura."

Good Lord, that voice. So deep. A bit rough, like the five o'clock shadow on his strong jaw.

"I am." Open-mouth gawking isn't appropriate with a man fifteen years my junior, so I consciously button my lips as he walks toward me.

The porch stairs groan beneath his feet. Not because the wood is weak or the workmanship shoddy. The opposite. I had the front porch refurbished last summer, it's plenty solid. But so is he. My stairs haven't been beneath such large feet before. Large feet, long legs, wide shoulders. My stairs aren't the only thing that could get used to being beneath that bulk.

"Hudson Andino," he says, extending one hand.

Sparks ripple through me the instant I accept his handshake. Each pump causes a tug between my legs. When was the last time I used my vibrator? A week ago? Longer? It's definitely coming out of the nightstand drawer tonight.

"Sorry for staring, I expected someone who looks like Seth and the other boys." I groan as the last word leaves my lips. "That makes it sound like I'm ancient. The other young men. No—just men. I need to start thinking of Seth's friends as men."

Hudson's eyebrows rise.

"That didn't come out the way I meant it," I say, heat blazing in my cheeks. "I'm not a cougar. Not that there's anything wrong with a mature woman getting involved with a younger man." Shit, and now he probably thinks I'm hitting on him. "Oh my God, you'd never know I'm a person who makes a living from words, would you?"

His dark eyes twinkle. "Seth mentioned you're an author."

"Yes, that's right." Given the rambling mess I've made of our first conversation so far, I'm not about to elaborate. If I mention *what* I write, it's likely to sound as if I'm propositioning my new tenant before he gets past the front door.

It's his fault. He's throwing me off with his manliness. I was expecting someone who reminded me of my son, not someone who could star in my late-night fantasies.

"Do you want help bringing things in?" I ask, reclaiming my hand before I have my first handshake-induced orgasm.

His eyes stay on my face as he shakes his head. "I only brought clothes over this trip. Seth said you'd be okay with me setting up some workout equipment, but I didn't want to overstep before we met."

"You want to set up your workout equipment." Nothing about this is going as anticipated. "I thought you'd want to set up your X-Box or PlayStation. You know, since you work with Seth, and all the other gamers."

"Yeah, video games aren't my thing. I'd rather do something physical."

So would I—with him. My mind is full of all kinds of physical things we could do.

He tracks my hand as I raise it to fidget with the top button of my scoop-neck t-shirt, where it sits at the center of my cleavage. "What about you?" he asks, meeting my eyes again. "Video games, or something more active?"

"Writing is a sedentary career, so I prefer to be active when I'm not working. I don't want to end up with writer's ass."

He smiles—and, oh, it's a nice one—then cocks his head to check out my backside. "Whatever you're doing now, keep doing it."

I laugh because it's the easiest response. But…did he just flirt with me? Maybe he's just a flirty guy. An appreciator of women in a general way. That's probably it. I'm a youthful forty-five, but Seth said Hudson is thirty. We're at different stages in life. He gave me a compliment, not a pickup line.

"Let's go inside and I'll show you where everything is."

"Sounds good." He shakes his head when I motion for him to head toward the front door. "Ladies first, Laura. Always."

Chronically undersexed me likes the sound of that. My vibrator is definitely getting a workout tonight.

I lead him through the house, pointing out all the obvious things. Main living room, the dining-room-turned-den, kitchen, a powder room. "There's a four-piece washroom upstairs, but only one." I glance over my shoulder while continuing the tour. "If you tell me your schedule, I'll make sure not to hold you up in the morning."

"I'm flexible. I'll fit it in whenever works best for you."

Oh, I bet he's flexible. As for fitting him in…morning,

noon, and night works for me. Good Lord, I need a date. Soon. Until then, I need to focus on being the nice landlady—my only role with this man.

"You're welcome to do laundry anytime, it's in the basement," I say as we enter the final room on the main floor. "And if you need anything, I'll probably be in here."

"This is a great space." He doesn't move away from me, but his gaze travels the room, taking in the vaulted ceiling, full-length windows on the rear wall, and my desk, where it faces the backyard. "Is this your office?"

"Yes. I don't mind if you enjoy the space too, as long as it's quiet enjoyment if I'm working."

He nods, the wheels turning behind his eyes. Whatever he's thinking, he keeps it to himself.

Something I also need to do. I'm not sure if he'll be staying with me for a week, a month, or longer. There's no true escape in this house, so my libidinous thoughts need to remain locked down, safely behind sealed lips.

"Back to the subject of your exercise equipment. Seth used the den at the front of the house as a gaming room. It's sitting empty, so you're welcome to it."

"That'd be great. You're sure you don't mind?"

"Not at all." I won't get the familiar sounds of video games I expected, but at least the house won't feel as empty. "I'll show you your bedroom, then leave you to settle in. Oh, and the rent is inclusive, so please help yourself to anything you want."

His lips curve into a smile that initiates a longing tug between my legs.

Am I sex-starved? Sadly, yes. Incredibly attracted to this man? Oh hell, yes. But I'm not desperate, delusional, or decrepit. I know a filthy-minded smile when I see one, and I'm definitely seeing one on Hudson's face.

I thought my new tenant would be a pseudo-son. Not

even close. He's going to be inspiration for my next romance novel instead.

---

# hudson

Alone behind a closed door, I sprawl out on the bed and exhale, long and low. Laura told me to make myself at home, but is it too soon to do that in the take-my-dick-out sense? Because I'd like to. Especially after following her up the stairs. That ass... I may have left a trail of drool up her perfectly polished hardwood.

When I asked the guys in my new office if anyone knew of a decent short-term rental, Seth's hand shot up like a keener in a high-school classroom. He's geeky and kind of naïve, but works hard with zero bullshit or drama. A good guy.

Hence, why I took his words at face value. "My mom has a spare room and she's lonely since I moved out. She's pretty cool for her age, and the house is clean. I'll see if she'd be willing to rent to you."

Lonely, cool for her age, keeps a clean house. That was Seth's description of his mother.

I was expecting somebody interchangeable with *my* mother. That's not who I got.

Laura is a fox. A beautiful woman with a smoking-hot body. The kind of woman who'd turn my head no matter where I saw her.

Yes, it would've been weird if my coworker had described his mother that way. But you'd think one of the other guys would've clued me in since they've all known Laura for years. Somebody should've taken me aside and mentioned that Seth's mom is fucking hot.

It's possible they haven't noticed. Based on their endless

conversations about video games, screens are getting all their attention, not women.

Fine by me. I'm more than willing to be the only guy looking at Laura. Touching her would be even better.

I peel off my t-shirt and shove my shorts down. My dick demands attention, so I wrap my fingers around it and slide my fist up and down. Lying in the semi-dark, I picture the heat in Laura's blue eyes when she checked me out on the porch. The way her lips parted and the tip of her tongue slid across her bottom lip.

I bet her lips are soft. I want to know if she sighs when she melts into a kiss, or if she moans. If she likes having her mouth fucked when she's on her knees, or if she likes to be in control when she gives head.

Eyes closed, I stroke my cock harder, faster. Pretend it's her lips wrapped around me, that's she's eagerly taking every inch. She's ready to swallow my load, but it's not enough—I need all of her. Fingers tangled in her sandy hair, I imagine guiding her to her feet. To the bed, where I spread her legs and bury my face between them. She's wet and ready, coming on my tongue, then begging me to bury my—

"Hudson," Laura's voice accompanies a light knock.

*Fuck.* "Just a sec." I whip my boxers and shorts into place, pushing my throbbing dick to one side as I hop off the bed. "Hey," I say, doing my best to look casual while opening the door.

"Sorry, I—" Pink floods her tanned face as her gaze travels over my bare chest, then lower, to the rock-hard salute of my dick, where it's tenting the front of my shorts.

I could tell her I was doing pushups. Maybe she'd believe I get super turned-on while working out. Fuck, do I even want her to believe that?

No excuses. I'm a man with a hard-on, and now she knows my dick works. No harm in that.

"What's up?" I raise my eyebrows when her gaze meets

mine. I'm not the only one caught in the act here, and I wink to let her know I don't mind having her eyes on my prize.

"I forgot to tell you there are lots of clean towels in the hall closet."

I track her hand as she fiddles with the neckline of her t-shirt again. The motion of her fingertips teasing that top button has my dick straining against my fly. *Open the button. Open them all.*

"And there's an empty hook in the bathroom. You can leave your damp towel there to dry."

"Will do." I brace my palms against the doorframe, giving my muscles a bit of extra flex when her attention shifts to my biceps. "Think I'll grab a shower now, if that's okay."

"Of course. Enjoy." More of that gorgeous blush rises to her cheeks as she realizes the implication of her final word, and its relativity to the raging hard-on pointed in her direction.

"I'll do that." I'm going to enjoy it until my knees buckle and my eyes roll back in my head. The smile I give her lets her know it, too. "Hey, Laura," I say as she turns in the second-floor hall.

She pauses, looks at me over her shoulder. "Yes?"

"If you don't have other plans, I'd like to take you to dinner."

"That's not necessary."

"If you mean I'm not obligated, you're right. I want to take you out. Get to know you, and vice-versa, if you're interested."

She takes a beat, then nods. "I am. I'll get changed while you shower."

"Great." I smile, doing my best to stay cool in front of this woman who's making me run hotter than I have in a long time. "I won't be long."

Her gaze drops to the front of my shorts again, and this time, it's *her* eyebrows that rise. She doesn't say a word, just gives me a cheeky smile before disappearing behind her bedroom door.

Doesn't matter if I take care of business in the shower, I'm going to be hard again as soon as I see her. This temporary living arrangement is nothing like I expected, because she's nothing like I expected. I'm either going to develop calluses on my right palm, or enjoy the hottest summer of my life.

# chapter two

. . .

### laura

STANDING BEFORE MY CLOSET, it's as if I'm in a movie, with an angel on one shoulder and a devil on the other.

"Choose something appropriate," whispers the angel. "Casual pants and a shirt."

"Wear a skimpy dress!" screams the devil. "You know you want to."

I reach for a pale-blue shirt, but my hand veers to a cherry-red sundress instead. The devil's right—I want to look sexy. A foolish choice? Possibly.

Hudson is my tenant. He invited me to join him for a meal so we can get better acquainted. My logical brain knows it's not a date. The part of my brain that has written nearly fifty romance books thinks, *but it could become a date.*

My muse refuses to be turned off, and Hudson's arrival has certainly turned her on. Seeing him shirtless and sporting a very obvious hard-on, how could I not be aroused? I don't *know* what he was doing behind the bedroom door, but I doubt he got that tentpole from unpacking.

He must have been in the midst of stroking himself off. And if he was, he's either perpetually horny, or the sparks between us affected him too. Maybe he has a thing for older women. Some men do, and I'm not a shriveled shrew, so I'm going with it.

In front of the floor-length mirror, I perform a visual assessment as I undress. The C-section scar is a silvery contrast to my summer-tanned skin. My thighs and abdomen are soft, but a lifetime of yoga and mostly clean eating have helped me maintain a decent physique. I'm comfortable in my skin. I certainly won't mind if Hudson wants to get comfortable inside me too.

My nipples are at attention when I remove my practical bra. Running my fingertips over them sends a tug of longing between my legs, the sensation amplifying when I tug the hard peaks. I need some release before I spend time in close proximity to Hudson.

I settle on the bed, leaning against the headboard. Legs spread, I slide a hand down my body. I pinch one nipple while rubbing my needy clit. A few seconds is all it takes to get close, but I don't want it to be over this quickly.

I lean sideways and open the nightstand drawer, withdrawing a dildo from my collection. It's long and girthy, with ridges and nubs. I nestle its head between my folds. Slide the tip deeper as I rub my clit again.

I'm close again within seconds. Hips arched, I rub harder and fill my pussy with the fake cock. Hudson's would-be cock, the one taunting me while he looked at me as if he wanted to throw me onto his bed and fuck me. God, I want him to fuck me. Every way humanly possible.

White flashes behind my eyelids as I come, my hips jerking upward to meet imaginary Hudson's thrusts. I should be satisfied, but the tingle is still there, demanding more. I roll onto my stomach and grind against my hand, riding out a second orgasm until I'm breathless.

Thumping from the spare bedroom—Hudson's room—reverberates through the wall as my heart returns to its normal pace. Dresser drawers closing, probably. Meaning I need to get ready.

There are some aspects of womanhood that I could do without, but when it comes to coming, women have the advantage. Multiple orgasms and no messy cleanup. I'm dressed, hair brushed and makeup freshened up within minutes. A pair of wedge-heeled espadrilles later, I'm ready for my non-date.

I don't have to go far on the main floor. Hudson is in the den, surveying the empty room. A navy t-shirt stretches across his wide upper back, molding over his shoulders and rounded biceps. His forearms are the stuff of fantasies, and his khakis hug his butt like a loving caress. Apparently, those two orgasms just scratched the surface, because my itch demands another scratching.

I'm pondering sneaking back upstairs when he turns to face me. "Thinking about where to put things?" I ask, pushing my naughty needs aside.

His gaze skates over my body, and when he meets my eyes, his glint with heat. "That's exactly what I'm thinking about."

I'm not imagining it, there's definitely mutual arousal.

The devil on my shoulder rubs its hands together. *We're having sex tonight.*

The angel on the other side gasps and clutches its pearls. *We cannot have intercourse with this man.*

If this evening goes well, I'm giving the devil permission to stuff a ball-gag in the angel's mouth. My dry spell has lasted too long. If Hudson wants to make my desert wet, I'm not turning him down. The angel on my shoulder can go to hell.

Hands in his pockets, he walks toward me, his dark-eyed, white-hot gaze still locked with mine. I'm not short, and I'm wearing heels, yet I have to tip my chin up to maintain eye contact once he's in my personal space.

"Does profanity offend you, Laura?"

"Not one fucking bit." My panties practically disintegrate when his lips curve into a wolfishly wicked smile.

"In that case, I won't settle for saying you look beautiful, I'll tell you you're sexy as fuck. Hope that's not too forward."

"Not when you say it."

The room temperature hasn't changed, but the air between us is thick with heat. His nostrils flare. There's no mistaking the scent of my arousal, made stronger by the orgasms I just had. With another man, I might make an excuse to move away, then rush to freshen up and rid myself of the embarrassing evidence. Only I can't recall a time I've been this turned on near a man who isn't actively working to make me this way.

"Ready to go?" he asks, breaking the electric silence.

"I'm ready for whatever you want." God, do I mean that literally.

"Let's start with dinner," he says, moving to my side. Eyes twinkling, he places a palm at the small of my back, then leans in close enough to tickle my cheek with his breath when he says, "You can let me know what you want for dessert later."

Oh, hallelujah. There's a sexual oasis in sight, and his name is Hudson. My time in the Sahara ends tonight.

---

# hudson

There aren't a ton of sit-down restaurants in a town this size. A total of two in the romantic category. On a Saturday evening in August, they're both packed. The Fischer Hotel's upscale dining room had a two-hour wait. A short walk brought us to The Undertow, Hope Harbor's only beachfront restaurant. Also lined up out the door.

When the hostess said there'd be a forty-five-minute wait, I offered to take Laura out of town, anywhere she wanted. We could call ahead to a restaurant in Hamilton or Kitchener. Hell, Toronto. She shook her head and smiled.

Standing on the wooden ramp for the better part of an hour didn't faze her. Maybe because she's lived here her entire life, and she's accustomed to the slow pace. Or maybe she's easygoing in general.

Either way, I like it. A lot. I also like the way the sun's twilight rays paint golden streaks in her hair. Hair I want to wrap around my fist as I guide her sexy lips onto my dick.

I've been staring at her mouth all evening. The sounds I heard that mouth making before we left the house are on replay in my mind. When I heard her moaning in the next room…fuck. Ear pressed to the wall, I wrapped my fist around my dick, stroking until my elbow thudded against the drywall.

I haven't attempted to hide my interest. I'm enjoying looking at her. I like her warm eyes. Her cute nose. The way the tip of her tongue peeks between her rosy lips as she raises the wineglass to her mouth. Her wide smile when she laughs. The sexy, closed-mouth smile she makes when I say something suggestive. Yeah, I really fucking like that.

Our casual conversation pauses as the entrées and drink refills arrive. Another local-winery chardonnay for Laura and a sparkling water for me. She only lives a few blocks up the hill and suggested we walk to dinner, but I declined. I wanted the opportunity to open her car door. To take her hand as she stepped out. That simple touch was electric.

She felt it too, I saw it in her wide eyes, heard it in the soft gasp that slipped from her parted lips. My need to get her naked is bordering on primal. An urge unlike anything I've felt before.

The caveman side of me is going to have to wait. I want to know all about this woman who's turned me inside out in the course of a couple hours.

"Tell me about your books," I say once the server's gone.

She arches an eyebrow while toying with the stem of her wineglass. "What did Seth tell you?"

Shit, there's a name I hoped to avoid tonight. I don't want her looking at me and thinking about her son. "Just that you're an author and spend most of your time writing."

Amusement plays across her face and she nods. "Good to know he's still embarrassed by my work."

"Being an author has to be one of the coolest professions around. Why would he be embarrassed?"

"Because I don't write books he'd want anyone to read. I'm a romance author."

"Romance books are pretty popular, aren't they?"

"Very. But mine aren't chaste. They're not the kind of stories you'd discuss around the water cooler." Her lucky glass gets to feel the press of her lips again as she tips her head for a long swallow of white wine. She captures a tagalong drop with her tongue, then leans forward while setting her near-empty glass on the table. "Seth would rather nobody knows the innerworkings of his mother's filthy mind."

All blood not required to keep me alive is now headed to my dick. "Then I'll be sure not to mention your books after I've enjoyed reading them."

Heads turn in our direction at the sound of her full-bodied laughter.

I lean in, pushing the centerpiece condiment basket aside to clear a path for when I reach for her hand, which is happening soon. "You have a great laugh."

"I'm enjoying using it tonight. Thank you for inviting me out to get to know each other."

I'm about to make my move, tell her my ulterior motives

for the invitation, when a man appears from behind me and stands by our table.

"Hey, Laura. Shelly and I heard your laugh from three tables over."

"How lucky for you and Shelly." She maintains a smile, but there's unmistakable bite in Laura's tone.

I straighten in my chair, shifting to ensure the guy sees the width of my shoulders—and the warning in my eyes. "Hudson Andino, the lucky man who gets to hear Laura's laughter up close and personal, all night long."

"Lance Swann," he says, accepting the hand I've extended and giving it an assertive squeeze. "The man who was up close and personal with Laura for twenty-two years."

"Until I stumbled upon the let's-get-a-hotel-room-after-the-office-Christmas-party messages between you and your twenty-six-year-old coworker," Laura says, rolling her eyes. "Stop trying to be the big dog in a yard you don't own anymore."

My assistance not required, I sit back and watch my gorgeous date put her ex in his place.

"And this puppy owns it now?" Lance asks boldly, stupidly, pointing at me.

Laura leans forward and swats his hand before I have an opportunity to grab it and bring the idiot to his knees—and tears. "*I* own my yard, Lance, and I'll let whomever I want play in it."

Fuck, she's sexy when she's fired up.

Since old Lancey-boy looks as if his head might pop off, it's safe to say he's fired up too. "That's why you're dressed like you wish you were still thirty, drawing attention to yourself, to put me in my place?"

"Yes, that's exactly it. Three years post-divorce, everything I do is about you." She reclines and waves him off. "Go back to your table. If you and your trophy wife can't handle that I'm having a good time, you can get a doggy bag and leave."

Lance doesn't take the suggestion, turning his focus on me instead. "You're Seth's friend."

"Coworker, not friend. He seems like a nice kid."

"Kid?" Lance snorts. "You're practically the same age. I had him fill me in on all your details before I let you move in."

"Before *you* let him move in?" Now it's Laura's angry, raised voice that's turning heads, not her beautiful laugh.

I stand, being sure to invade Lance's personal space as I glare. "I'm going to say this once, politely, for Laura's sake. You need to shut up and fuck off. Now."

"You think telling me to shut up and fuck off is polite?"

"Compared to *making* you by putting my fist in your face, yes."

Lance makes the wise choice and walks away, but I don't move until I'm sure his decision sticks. Once he's seated across from a brunette whose face I can't see, I settle on my chair.

"Sorry for overstepping," I say, reaching for her hand. Not the reason I wanted to initiate physical contact, but she curls her soft fingers around mine, so I'll take it. "You're obviously a woman who doesn't need a man to rescue her."

"Thank you. And you're right, I'm capable of taking care of myself." She withdraws her hand and unrolls her flatware from a napkin, a fresh smile on her face as she scoops a forkful of today's featured entrée. "I won't lie, though. Part of me loved the novelty of a big, strong man jumping up to protect me."

"It shouldn't be a novelty. The man in your life should always be ready and willing to defend you, in whatever way necessary." I grin when her eyebrows rise. "That's right, I just appointed myself the man in your life."

Her laugh is lighter than the warm summer breeze rippling across the beachfront restaurant's wide, outdoor-dining area. "I suppose you get the title by default since you're the only man I'll see on a daily basis for the next while. Have you looked at any houses since moving from Toronto?"

I let her *default* comment slide. Now's the wrong time to push for more with a woman I've only known a few hours. But there will be more between us. A lot more. I felt the click the minute we met. "I've seen two properties. The first one didn't interest me and the second was sold before I got my offer in. Nothing else has listed since. My realtor suggested I look in Simcoe, because the office is there, but I want to be on the water. Or close enough to walk to it, like your place is."

She nods while chewing. "There's never much for sale here during the summer. If you can stand living with me until the tourist season ends, you'll have better options."

"Staying with you won't be a hardship." But I will be hard. All the damn time. "Your ex is an idiot, by the way. Any man who cheats is a douchebag, but a man who'd cheat on a beautiful, intelligent woman like you has to be the stupidest asshole around."

"Lance would tell you he didn't cheat. That he was flattered by the attention of a pretty twenty-six-year-old and made a mistake, but they were 'only texting.'"

"I'm glad you didn't fall for that. Doesn't matter if his dick was involved, he broke his commitment, and that's cheating."

"That's refreshing to hear that from a man."

"We're not all dogs who stray. Some of us are loyal."

Sunlight bounces off her hair as she smiles and shakes her head. "You're either one hell of a catch, or a very smooth bullshitter."

"Choose door number one. You won't be disappointed."

She sets her fork aside and picks up her glass, surveying me over the rim before draining the remaining chardonnay. "You're going to have a lineup outside that door. There aren't many houses on the market in Hope Harbor, but there are plenty of single women."

"Not interested in a lineup. I'm a one-woman man."

"Then she'll be a lucky young woman when you find her." She gives me a tightlipped smile while moving her napkin from lap to table. "Excuse me while I use the ladies' room. Unless you want dessert, I'm ready to get the check and go." She's gone before I can answer, robbing me of the chance to tell her *she's* the dessert I want.

I'm on my feet—because a real man stands when a woman does—and the position gives me a great view of her shapely body as she walks. I watch until she disappears inside the building, but I don't sit yet. There's something I need to do.

Lance stiffens as I approach, his beady eyes shifting from me to the restaurant's door, but never to my table. Because he knows Laura's not at the table. The bastard watched her go inside.

His wife smiles up at me, clearly oblivious to what happened when Lance left their table earlier. She's attractive, but compared to fiery Laura, she's a dim flame. That's about the nicest thing I can come up with for this woman who pursued a married man.

I don't do false pleasantries, so I ignore her and focus on Lance. "You're never going to speak to Laura that way again. What she wears, how loud she laughs, who she spends time with, or anything else about her are none of your business. You made the mistake of choosing this life over one with Laura. Now live with it, and keep your jealous shit to yourself."

"I'm not jealous." His bark of contempt might fool his wife, but not me.

"Lance…" Shelly glances back and forth between us. "Who is this, and what is he talking about?"

No way I'm giving Lance a chance to answer. "I'm the man who's going to treat Laura the way she deserves, which includes respecting her choices, appreciating her beautiful, sexy perfection, and satisfying her in ways your husband never did." *Now* I smile at Lance's gape-mouthed wife.

"Better keep him on a leash, Shelly. Some dogs will wander out of the yard if the gate's open, even a crack."

Laura's presence pings my internal radar the moment she steps out of the restaurant.

"There's my lady," I say, rapping the tabletop before walking away without further words. I'm not wishing them a good night because I honestly hope they don't have one. I signal the server on my way to Laura, withdrawing my wallet as I reach our table.

She's cheekily silent while I settle the check. "Apparently, I can't leave you alone," she says, as I tuck my credit card away.

"I'd rather you didn't. Here or at home." I span her lower back with my palm, then guide her toward the door.

"Dare I ask why you were at their table?"

"Just reminding Lance that he's out of your life, and I'm going to fill every hole he left in bigger, better ways."

A beautiful, carefree laugh—like the one that drew her asshole ex-husband to our table—bursts from her smiling mouth, filling the evening air. "You didn't say that."

"Not exactly."

"Oh good."

"But I did say I'm going to satisfy you in all the ways he never did."

Her eyes widen and her bottom lip falls open. "Oh my God."

"He didn't look happy about it. Safe to say he still has feelings for you."

"Maybe so, but his expression was probably about his feelings of inadequacy in the satisfaction department."

"He couldn't get it up? As much as I already hate the guy, part of me feels bad for any man who can't get it up."

"Don't feel bad, he could get it up. He just didn't want to do much with it. Let's just say, he liked to use the front door, but didn't want to go downtown, and had no interest in taking the back way." She laughs as we reach the car. "God, I can't believe I'm telling you this."

I resisted holding her hand on the walk because she kept a buffer between us. Now that we've reached the car, I close that gap and bracket her between my arms and the passenger door. "And I can't believe any heterosexual male wouldn't want to enjoy every single inch of you, over and over, with his fingers, tongue, and cock. Because I sure as hell do."

"Hudson…" Her voice is low and breathy as she flattens her palms on my chest, sending a jolt straight to my dick. "As much as I want to take you up on that very tempting offer, I can't."

"Because of your ex?"

"Indirectly, yes. Hope Harbor is a small town, and I'm not going to be the talk of it, the way Lance was when he went public with a girlfriend young enough to be his daughter. I'm not interested in being tagged as a rebound cougar, even for what I'm sure would be some mind-blowing sex."

Maybe it's a dick move, but I hold my ground when she applies pressure to my chest. "It's a completely different situation. We're single, mature, consenting adults with fifteen years between us. That's nothing at our ages."

"Unless you're a forty-five-year-old woman and everyone's gossiping about the time you were banging a thirty-year-old while he rented a room in your house."

"So, you're anticipating the fallout from a breakup before I've kissed you on our first date."

"I'm focusing on self-preservation. A must when you live in a town this size. It's not the same as a city like Waterloo, where you're one among several hundred thousand people. Or when you're early in a career that could take you anywhere, like yours just has."

This time when she presses my pecs, I drop my hands to my sides and step back. "Sounds like your mind is made up."

"It is. We were never meant to go on a date. You're not

what I expected, and I indulged in a couple hours of 'what if' fantasy, but I need to be sensible going forward. I planned to have a temporary tenant, and that's all our relationship is going to be."

Like hell. But this isn't the time or place to show her what we can be. What I know in my gut we will be. Instead, I open her door. Hold her gaze as she settles on the creamy leather, then exhale when her soulful blue eyes disappear from view behind the dark-tinted window.

I'll take her home. Say goodnight without kissing her. Lie in bed without touching her. For now. But not forever.

# chapter three

. . .

## laura

METAL CLINKING carries from two rooms over as Hudson racks the barbell above his weight bench. After two weeks with Hudson in the house, I know the sound well. I can visualize the activity.

Mid-sentence, I close my eyes and picture him. He's shirtless, lying on his back, muscular thighs parted, feet planted on either side of the bench. The knob of his cock is visible through his thin athletic shorts, his broad chest rising and falling as he catches his breath between sets. Yes, I'm working from memory. Yes, I ogled him while he worked out the other day. No, I'm not ashamed. Yes, I'm hornier than ever before.

Metal clinks again, pulling me from my visualization. Heavy exhaling becomes grunting. He's doing chest presses. Glorious chest presses.

I've heard more masculine grunting in the past fourteen days than in the twenty-two years I spent with Lance. My ex-husband was never a physical guy. He didn't exert himself during sports, handyman chores, nor in our bedroom. Lance was never overweight, he was just a shapeless man who preferred to sit rather than move. Sit at the office. Sit on our couch. Sit on his side of our bed, donning his pajamas before giving me a passionless goodnight kiss.

I was eighteen and green as a spring day when we began dating. Lance was twenty-one, and I believed myself the luckiest girl in town, drawing the eye of "a cute older guy." He was my first lover. I accepted everything he did—and didn't do—as the norm. When our bland, beginner sex resulted in an accidental pregnancy, he proposed immediately.

After Seth was born, Lance was happy for me to be a stay-at-home mother, raising our son and "dabbling at that writing thing." I thought I'd hit the jackpot in terms of happily ever after.

Life was idyllic, aside from our once-a-week sex that left me wanting rather than satisfied. That's what secret vibrators and midday masturbation are for, right? My husband loved me. What else could matter?

Then I hit my thirties. My desire to write coming-of-age love stories with tender kisses and tentative touches waned as my libido went into overdrive. I took a pseudonym, dipped my toes into adult romance, found my new tribe, and fell madly in love with steamy sex scenes. My backlist of dirty books grew. So did my bank account. Readers sent emails thanking me for jumpstarting their love lives. And I felt like the world's biggest fraud.

How could I accept praise for my scorching sex scenes when no matter what I tried, I couldn't convince my husband to turn my literary imaginings into reality? The best he'd give me were a couple of light licks before boarding the missionary bus.

Still, I was mostly happy. Content with the majority of my life. I assumed Lance felt the same way, since he controlled the map of our lives. It was good enough.

Until the day I used his tablet while mine updated, and saw him exchanging messages with Shelly, right before my

Fleshing It Out

eyes. Syncing across devices isn't a good idea if you're making plans to screw someone other than your wife.

In the years since my divorce, I've dated four men, and had sex with two. Guy number one must've taken the same how-not-to-satisfy-a-woman class as Lance. Guy number two proved that real-life men *could* compete with the fictional ones—in the bedroom. Too bad he was a jerk outside the sheets.

Maybe it's unrealistic to expect reality to deliver everything I've written into a fantasy man. Someone handsome, hard-bodied, take-charge, but also sensitive. A man who's intelligent enough to hold a conversation, makes me laugh, treats me with respect, but also wants to fuck me like the bad, bad girl I long to be…

Only, he's not fictional. My fantasy man exists, two rooms over. If only Hudson were my age, or in the latter half of his thirties.

It's easy to forget he's only thirty. That I've only known him a couple weeks. When he walks through the door, there's energy between us, like those super-strong magnets that shoot across a table to connect. Minus the physically connecting, of course, since I put the kibosh on that our first evening together. But the hum is always there. So is great conversation and easy, relaxed laughter. We'd be a great couple. If we could be a couple…

His workout grunts—which could easily pass for sexy-time grunts—continue in the other room. I can't concentrate on writing this narrative scene while he's making those sounds. I hate writing out of order, but screw it, I'll come back and finish this part later.

Hands on the keyboard, I greenlight my muse. She wants to write sex, so that's what I write. And write, and write, and write, as if my fingers are on fire. Page after page of sex so deliciously filthy, my body is buzzing.

It's the aroma from the kitchen that snaps me from my writing trance. I look up and find him watching. He's leaning against the archway, muscular arms crossed over his shirtless chest. Smiling at me. No, smiling doesn't adequately describe it. He's *smoldering* at me.

With the state I'm in from writing a hot-and-heavy, multi-orgasmic sex scene, it's a miracle I don't lunge across the room, drop to my knees, and suck every drop of smolder he's got.

"You're cooking?" I ask instead, because I'm a mature woman. But I'm also me, so I can't resist cocking an eyebrow and adding, "Since you're not wearing a shirt—again—I hope you're not making something with hot grease that could splatter."

He might as well be zapping me with a remote-controlled vibrator when he chuckles. "Pineapple chicken with rice pilaf. No grease involved."

"Sounds great, thank you." Is it coincidence that he chose to cook with pineapple? Probably. Writing dirty romance changes the perspective on everything. Pineapple can simply be a delicious food, it doesn't have to be a tool to make semen taste better. Not that I'll know if it works. God, I'd love to be his taste tester.

I push the sex-starved thought aside. "Let me save and close my file, then I'll help."

He shakes his head. "I've got it under control. You've made dinner nearly every night since I got here, I'm overdue to take a turn. Plus, you're on a roll over there."

"Sometimes I get in a good groove."

"I noticed." He pushes away from the wall, winking before returning to the kitchen.

There's no way I can continue writing an anal-sex scene starring a tall, dark-haired man when my inspiration for the hero is within earshot, and apparently, tuned in to the sound of my clicking keys. God help me if he shows more interest and asks what has me typing so fast.

I head toward the kitchen, where my bottom lip nearly

hits the floor. "Oh my God." Forget pineapple chicken, I'm having buns for dinner. Firm, round, squeezable buns.

Hudson turns to face me, and I force my gaze from the front of his white boxer briefs. But it's hard. Because all I'm thinking about is how *hard* it could be.

To prevent anyone from accidentally reading my work, I've always positioned my desk to face the room, not the wall. Sitting behind my oversized monitor, I'd only had a view of Hudson from his chiseled chest up. Now, I see practically everything. Including the outline of something mouthwateringly long and thick.

"You're in your underwear."

"Would you rather I wasn't?" he asks, hooking his fingers under the waistband.

"Yes. I mean no. Oh my God, there's no right way to answer."

"Yeah, there is. Tell me you want them off." Smoldering smile still firmly in place, he draws the white fabric down until it catches on the head of his cock. Given its size, that's not far.

"I can't say that." The angel on my shoulder gives me a good-girl pat while the devil wails in disappointment. *Me too, little devil. Me too.*

"All right." He snaps the waistband back into place. Returns to the business of cooking as if this isn't the least bit unusual.

I should take the olive branch—or whatever this is—but my turned-on-from-writing-sex side is too discombobulated. "You're cooking in a pair of leaves-nothing-to-the-imagination underwear, and all you have to say is *all right*?"

He sets the spatula on a spoon rest, then moves toward me with the presence of a muscular jungle cat. "You said you can't tell me to take off my boxers, not that you want me to leave them on."

"Same thing." My voice is inappropriately breathy, but he's so close, it's a miracle I can breathe at all.

He shakes his head. "Two very different things and you know it. I want to be with you in every imaginable way, Laura. Have since the minute I met you. I'll keep the door open, but I won't push you through it. When you're ready, you'll let me know."

I love that he respects my boundaries. Right now, though, I wish he'd disrespect them. Just a little. Because I can't invite him through that open door, no matter how much I want to. "I told you why we can't act on our physical attraction."

"And there's that word *can't* again." He winks one twinkling, mischievous eye, then ignites a frenzy of sparks as he gently cups my face. "Forget *can't* for a minute. We'd set the bed on fire, that much is undeniable. But there's more to it. A connection. I know you feel it too."

"How do you know?"

"Because of the connection."

I can't help laughing at his cheekiness and accompanying grin, and when he threads his fingers through my hair, I don't resist leaning in to his touch.

"Don't you want to see where this could go?"

One word would nip this thing in the bud. It's not the word I say. "Yes. But wanting to doesn't mean I can. See, I didn't say *can't* this time." It's a shitty attempt at a joke, barely deserving of the half-assed smile it nets. "How long until dinner's ready? Do I have ten minutes to pop out for a bottle of wine?"

"I picked some up earlier. It's in the fridge."

"Great," I say, when it's the opposite. That trip to the store would've given me time to regroup. To fortify myself against this thoughtful, sexy man who's taken up residence behind my defenses. In my heart. "I'll pour some while you finish with dinner."

He wraps his arm around my waist when I try to move away. "Do something for me?"

"Get you a pair of pants?"

He pulls me tighter, his easygoing smile loosening the knot in my chest. "Hell, no. That'd make it easier for you to fight what's happening between us."

"Nothing's happening. We're temporarily sharing the house. Having great conversation, laughs, and meals together." Even as I stand firm with my words, my body's going pliant against his. "We're becoming friends."

"We're already friends, and you know it's more than that." His eyes are soulful gateways to everything he's offering to give me. He leans in, presses his lips to my hair, then strokes my cheek before moving away to tend our dinner. "I'm looking at a house tomorrow. I'd like you to go along, give your opinion on it."

"That's the thing you want me to do?"

Glancing over his shoulder, he nods. "If you have time. I know you're on a deadline."

"Of course, I'll go." The end to perpetually yearning for someone I can't have may be in sight. This should be good news, yet my stomach is in knots and pressure is building behind my eyes. "How exciting."

"Hoping so." Broad back to me, he turns off the stove, then serves food onto two plates. "Ready when you are," he says, carrying our dinner to the table.

"Great." Fake smile in place, I collect two glasses from the cabinet and duck into the fridge for the wine. I'm expecting white because it's chilling. Also because we're having chicken, and in two weeks living together, I've learned Hudson is a man who knows how to pair. I'm not expecting to find a bottle of my favorite local chardonnay with a handwritten note tented over the neck.

*Every time I drink this wine I'll be picturing you in that red dress, smiling and laughing. The most beautiful woman I've ever seen. The one I can't wait to look at across the dinner table every night.*

I know it's wrong, but I hope the house he looks at tomorrow is terrible. Or already sold by the time we get there. I can't have everything I want with Hudson, but I'm not ready for him to move on. The trouble is, I don't know if I ever will be.

# chapter four

### . . .

## hudson

I KNOW she wanted me to kiss her. In the kitchen when I had her in my arms. At the table, as she pressed her bare knee against mine. On the couch afterward, her hand casually brushing my quadriceps, making my cock hard as fuck for three hours straight. I've never wanted to kiss a woman that badly in my life.

Knowing she wants me isn't enough. Some guys would take the physical cues and make a move. I need her to tell me. Say my name and invite me through that door I've kicked open. Kissing her once, fucking her once, won't be enough. I know it without doing it. Once we get started, there's not going to be an end.

It'll happen. Until it does, I'm in erotic purgatory.

Every night, my dick is hard before she reaches the end of her, "I'm heading to bed" statement. The dick knows. Doesn't matter whether it's nine o'clock or midnight, or what I'm doing, I'm right behind her. Because Laura doesn't go to sleep right away. Not until she's had a few orgasms in the room beside mine.

Pretty sure she's unaware how much sound travels in this house. Or maybe she knows the walls are paper-thin, but thinks she's being quiet enough. She's not.

I hear the buzz of her vibrator. The snapping lid of her lube. Every hitch in her breath. Every moan as she's fucking herself with the thick dildo she accidentally left in the bathroom one day. Every softly panted plea when she comes. And comes again. And again.

Every. Fucking. Night.

Including right fucking now.

Tonight must've really gotten to her too, because she's already come three times, and she's still going. Louder than normal. Tonight, it's not just the hum of her voice, it's words.

"All the way in my ass…"

Jesus, is she fucking herself in the ass with that thing? I'll give her that, only so much better. I jerk my dick faster, fire racing up from my balls as she moans on the other side of the wall. I clamp down on the facecloth I shoved in my mouth, fighting my desperate need to unload until I hear her make that special sound. Her sound. My sound, because it's for me. About me.

The sound she's making now.

The wadded terrycloth absorbs my groan as I coat my pumping fist with a volcano of cum. I stroke until it's too sensitive, then spit out the cloth and lie there, chest heaving as I catch my breath. One of these nights, she's going to invite me in. When we come together, I'll be inside her.

Tonight's not that night, unfortunately, so I reach for the towel beside my bed. Not there. Fuck, where is it? I flick on the bedside lamp, and glance around the room. No towel anywhere.

She must've taken it when she did laundry earlier. She did instruct me to hang my towel on a bathroom hook to dry. Shit. There's too much jizz for me to get up and grab a t-shirt from the dresser. I'd rather not explain a trail of crusty spots on the carpet, so, Plan C it is. I remove the pillowcase and use it to take care of jizzness, then pull on boxers, open the door, and run smack into Laura.

She shrieks, the whites of her eyes nearly glowing from the moonlight coming through the hall window.

"Sorry." My hands are on her waist. An instinctual move when I bumped into her, but I don't take them away. "Fuck it, I'm not sorry," I say, tugging her against me and claiming her mouth the way I've wanted to do for two long, hard-dick weeks.

She gasps against my lips, then opens. Sucks my tongue into her minty-sweet heaven. Whatever toy she just used thuds to the floor as she wraps her arms around my neck and crushes her sweet tits against my chest.

Doesn't matter that I just came, I'm hard again. I palm her ass, slide my fingers beneath the top edge of whatever tiny panties she's not going to be wearing for long. I groan at the slickness in the valley of her perfect peach. "Fuck, sweetheart, is that lube? You *were* fucking yourself in the ass in there, weren't you?"

"You could hear me?"

"I hear you every night."

She inhales sharply as she backs out of my arms. "Oh my God, do you know what that means?"

"That I'm simultaneously the luckiest and unluckiest man on the planet? Yeah."

There's no laugh, nudge, or any other playful response. Just pacing in the semi-dark hall, while covering her mouth and shaking her head. "No wonder Seth couldn't wait to move out. He had to listen to his mother masturbating for the last four years. Oh my God, oh my God."

Nothing like discussing her kid—my geeky coworker—to kill the mood. Right now, my lady needs something else, and I'm still the man to give it to her. "That's not why he moved out," I say, cupping her shoulders to still her.

"But if you heard me, he would have too. I'm the worst mother ever, I've probably scarred him for life."

"You're not, and I'm positive you didn't."

"How? How can you be so sure?" She's so fucking beautiful, staring up at me with wide-eyed vulnerability.

There's nothing I wouldn't do to protect her. Nothing. Burn bridges, knock down assholes, whatever she needs, including giving her peace of mind, even if it costs me.

"Sweetheart, I heard you because I'm listening. I can't help myself. Every minute we're sharing space, I'm tuned in to you. That probably makes me sound like a pervy stalker, and if you don't want me here anymore, I'll pack my things right now."

"I don't think you're a pervy stalker, and I don't want you to leave."

Thank fuck for that, because despite my offer, I would've done whatever it took to stay right here. "Also, Seth's a gamer whose setup was on the main floor. I've seen the headphones those guys wear. There's no way he could've heard anything. He's an adult with a good full-time job. He moved out because it was time for him to take the next step in life."

"You're right." Exhaling, she melts against me when I pull her into my arms. "Thank you."

"I'm here for you. Whatever you need," I say, sliding my hand lower, to her perfect ass. "I'm here to give it to you."

The air charges when she tilts her head and meets my gaze. "I wish I could take you up on that."

"You can. Say the word and I'll make every wish into reality." My rock-hard dick is sandwiched between us, and when she runs her soft hands over my skin, I thrust my hips out of base, instinctive need. "You have no idea how much I want you."

"Then you'd better show me," she whispers. "Show me all night long."

The beast roars inside me. I scoop her into my arms,

claiming her mouth as I carry her to her room. Moonlight floods through two windows, bathing the space in silvery light. I lay her out on the bed, strip away the scraps of material covering her soft curves. Tits made for my mouth. Thighs that're going to feel so fucking good wrapped around me.

"Don't." I catch her hand when she places it over the scar on her lower abdomen. "Everything about you is sexy and beautiful. I want all of you, every single inch."

She stretches her arms above her head, arches her back, and spreads her shapely legs. "Take every part of me." Her tongue slides over her lips as I shuck my boxers. "That promise you made to fill all the holes in my life…I want you to make good on it."

"I can do a hell of a lot better than 'good,' sweetheart." I gather her wrists in one hand. Cover her with my body and kiss her pretty mouth while grinding my cock on her clit.

She's shaking beneath me within seconds, her hands straining against the bond of my fingers. "Please…" She pants the word between kisses. "Please."

"I'll make you come, but I'm not letting you go, sweetheart. Not now, not ever." I crush my lips to hers, stroking my tongue into her hot mouth as I rock my dick faster and harder over her clit.

Her moan vibrates through me as she comes, and it takes every shred of self-control not to slide home right now. She needs to know she's safe with me first. That I'll do whatever she needs to take care of her.

I release her hands, sparks skittering through me when she twines her arm behind my head. "Been waiting to hear that up close for two weeks." I drop another kiss on her smiling lips. "I'm going to make you come so many times, sweetheart."

"Just so you know…I'm clean, and I'm on the Pill. Figured we should get the practical stuff out of the way, even if it's not sexy."

"Everything about you is sexy, including your brain. I'm safe too. Got checked out after my last relationship ended, and I had a vasectomy five years ago. But I've got condoms in the other room if you want to use them."

Hair fanned on the pillow, she tilts her head, but doesn't ask the question I've been answering since I had the snip. She just says, "I trust you."

Important words from a woman who's been on the shitty end of infidelity. Something she'll never have to worry about with me. But that's a promise for another time.

Right now, it's time to make good on a different promise. One more taste of her soft lips, then I head south. Her pulse hammers beneath my mouth as I inhale near her earlobe. "You always smell so good. I get hard every time you're close enough that I can catch your scent."

"You must be perpetually hard, because you seem to end up in my personal space a lot."

I chuckle and work my way down, slipping my hand between her legs as I trace circles around her nipple with my tongue. "It's no accident when I'm close to you. I can't stay away."

Her breath catches when I scrape my teeth over her nipples, one, then the other. And when I slide two fingers through her slick heat, she tips her hips up and moans.

"I could make you come again, like this." I roll my fingers over her clit. "But I'm going to fuck you after you come, and I need to eat your sweet pussy first."

"God, yes, get down there," she says, playfully pushing the top of my head.

"With pleasure." I settle between her soft thighs, using my shoulders to nudge them wide. My cock is a battering ram, and I thrust against the bed as I bury my face in her pussy.

She's spicy-sweet perfection, and I can't get enough. Arms looped under her hips, I pull her closer. Hold her in place while I eat her out as if she were my last fucking meal.

Panting above me, she grabs my head, her fingernails raking my scalp. My rhythm goes to shit as she grinds onto my tongue. Then the sexy moan I've been jerking off to daily fills my ears like the sweetest fucking music.

I lap at her, slow and gentle, until the last ripple subsides. When her hands fall to my shoulders, I climb up her body, and kiss her irresistible lips. "Going to do that again after I fuck you."

"Yes, please, to both."

"Such good manners," I say, nudging her pussy with the head of my cock. That's the end of my joking, and my restraint. I fill her in one thrust, holding still when I'm buried to the balls. "Jesus, you're tight." And so fucking right.

Legs around my back, she pulls me deeper. Pulls me in with her eyes too. I could get lost in her so fucking easily. Lips sealed together, I stroke into her perfect pussy. Deep. So fucking deep.

She makes an indescribable sound, her breath hitching as she digs her nails into my butt. I know what she needs, so I give it to her. Change the angle, stroke her G-spot, grind on her clit while I'm buried in her hot pussy.

*"Hudson."* My name rides her breath as she bucks beneath me, coming around my cock.

Flames lick at the base, but I'm not ready for this to end. "You're so fucking sexy, baby. Fucking perfect. Tell me what you want so I can give it to you."

"Flip me over and..." She pulls her bottom lip between her teeth, her eyes blazing with need. "Fuck my ass."

It's a miracle I don't come just from hearing her say it. I kiss her again, then pull out, groaning at the sight of her when she rolls onto her stomach.

"There's lube in the nightstand."

Good thing, because I plan to bury every inch in her beautiful ass.

She watches over her shoulder, not taking her eyes off me

as I coat my dick. A soft gasp leaves her parted lips when I drizzle lube down her valley, her eyelids fluttering closed as I massage it over her rim.

I breach her tight ring with the tip of one finger. She groans and pushes back, taking it all, but given what she's told me about her marriage, I need to be sure. My dick's a hell of a lot bigger than my finger.

"Feel good?"

"Yes, but it's not enough."

I grunt and slide my finger free. "Don't worry, sweetheart, I've got more than enough to satisfy you." I add more lube to my palms, then massage her cheeks and pussy until she's relaxed. Until she's humming every time I stroke my finger over her pucker.

"Spread your ass for me," I say, taking my dick in hand. "Fuck, you're so sexy, lying there, offering your sweet ass to me."

"It's yours."

"Fucking right, it's mine." Fist curled around my dick, I position the throbbing head against her rim. And press. I groan as her body resists and accepts at the same time. The sight of my cock disappearing into her ass is almost too much, but I can't *not* watch.

She moans as I push deeper, and her hands slide from her cheeks. They're underneath her now. She's rubbing her clit, I can feel the motion of her fingers by my balls. And she's getting close, I hear it in her hitched breathing. Feel it as she grinds her hips downward, onto her hand.

"Fuck, baby, you're squeezing me out."

"Then you'll have to fuck me harder."

Permission to fuck her harder taken. Hands curled around her hips, I push deeper. Deeper. Until there's nothing left to give because every inch of my dick is buried. "Fuck, baby, fuck," is all I can manage as I withdraw and fill her again. Again.

Fleshing It Out

The sexiest moan in the goddamn world fills my head as she bears down, riding her hand.

"Fuuuuck…" I throw my head back and let go. Every pulse, every throbbing fucking second amplified by the tight squeeze of her ass as she comes.

"Oh my God," she says, after I've slipped from her body and rolled us to our sides. "That was better than anything I've ever written."

"Damn high praise from the Peachy Queen."

She turns to face me so quickly, I have to think fast to avoid a knee to the groin. "How do you know that nickname?"

"Your socials are public. You've got a rep for your hot anal scenes."

"Oh God." It's too dark to see their color, but her cheeks are hot when she buries her face against my chest. "How much did you see?"

"Everything." I could give her a break, but where's the fun in that? "Including your recent 'book inspiration' posts."

"Noooo…"

"Oh, yeah." I tighten my arms around her, laughing when she kitten-struggles against my hold. "Love your newest hero's name. Judson has a nice ring to it."

"Kill me now," she says, her groan spurring me to deeper laughing.

"Can't. Me and your other faithful followers need you to finish writing Judson's book first. I need to know if he gets to eat Maura's sweet peach, like the teaser implies. I know I'm rooting for the guy."

Her head snaps up, those beautiful eyes of hers meeting mine in a bug-eyed stare. "You can't read my book."

"Can and will, sweetheart. Just like I can and did with a bunch of the others. You write one hell of a story."

"I knew I should've hid my paperback copies while you were staying here."

"I didn't read your copies. I bought my own. Have to support my favorite author."

"You're very sweet," she says, scooting up to kiss me.

"I'm very crazy about you. About everything you are, and everything you do." Maybe it's too much, more than she's ready to hear. She'll have to get used to it, because there's a lot more I plan to say.

She doesn't answer, but this time, when she burrows against me, it's a snuggle, not an attempt to hide. "Did you really get a vasectomy when you were twenty-five?"

"I did."

"Was it for health reasons?"

"No," I say, feeling my defenses rising, as they always do during this conversation with a woman. "Strictly personal choice."

"That's young. I'm surprised the doctor didn't try talking you out of it."

"They asked if I was sure, and I was. Still am."

"Do you hate kids?" she asks, tipping her head back to meet my gaze.

"No, not at all. I just don't want any. Before the snip, I was engaged. I'd been completely honest about what I wanted out of life, and she said she was good with it. Two months before the wedding, she told me she was pregnant. It wasn't accidental, and wasn't a mutual decision. She thought once I found out, I'd realize I really did want to be a father, and our happily ever after would include our bundle of joy."

"What happened?"

"I ended the relationship. Had a lawyer draw up support papers. I told her I'd take care of them financially, that I'd coparent because it was the right thing to do for the child, but I didn't want that life 24/7."

"Wow, that's—"

"Cold? Heartless? A total asshole move and you can't believe you just slept with such a son-of-a-bitch?"

"None of the above. You loved her and had a future planned. It must've broken your heart when she betrayed you."

Of course, Laura would understand. Broken trust is the core of betrayal, whether it happens via text messages or pregnancy.

"I did, and it did. But I also felt like a cold, heartless asshole."

"And I felt like an oblivious idiot who might be overreacting, like my husband accused me of, when I ended two decades of marriage over a thread of flirtatious text messages. We feel however we feel, and we get to feel however that is."

"You're amazing."

"I have my moments of greatness." Her light laughter is a prize, and she smiles when I catch her hand and bring it to my lips for a kiss.

"Every moment with you is great."

Palm cupping my cheek, she looks into my eyes. Into my soul, so fucking tenderly. "Do you have a son, or a daughter?"

"Neither. She had a miscarriage at eight weeks. She was distraught, I was relieved. The rest is history."

"You know the good thing about history? It brings us to the present. And I'm pretty happy with my present."

"Me too, sweetheart." I tighten my embrace, stroking her hair as her breathing settles into a long, deep, sleepy pattern. Careful not to disturb her, I cover us with a blanket. Press a kiss to her head. "Good night, beautiful."

She mumbles something indiscernible, sighs softly, and slings her leg over mine. I'm pretty fucking happy with my present too.

## chapter five
. . .

### laura

"IT'S SO great of you to come with Hudson." Alana smiles, her round face full of phony friendliness as she unlocks the house.

Beside me, Hudson coughs to cover a laugh. I know exactly what he's thinking—about how great it was when I *came* with him thirty minutes ago, while he fucked me for the second time this morning. He's not wrong, it was great. But nobody can know about the amazing sex we're having. We can't let anyone catch a whiff of our new connection.

He doesn't know Alana Martin isn't just the most go-getting real estate agent in town, she's also one of the nosiest, most loudmouthed gossips. I'll clue him in later. For now, I'd like to elbow him in his toned six-pack. But I won't.

That kind of contact would stir Alana's curiosity. It's bad enough that she commented on my presence for this viewing. God help me if she even begins to do the math.

"Hudson wanted an unbiased female opinion," I say, as Alana ushers us into the foyer.

"No, I wanted your opinion." He doesn't just follow me

Fleshing It Out

in, he does so with his palm against the small of my back. A gesture that doesn't go unnoticed by his hawk-eyed realtor.

I'm tempted to explain it off as traditional, gentlemanly behavior. But anything I say will only draw more attention to the physical contact. The best I can do is put a buffer between us, and keep it there.

Hudson doesn't make that easy. Every step of Alana's guided tour, he's at my side, close enough that our shoulders brush. Close enough for him to graze my hand with his fingertips while we're inspecting kitchen cupboards. Closer than a platonic acquaintance should be.

Every subtle touch ignites more sparks between us. I should be checking the house over with a critical eye. Instead, I'm picturing all the places he can fuck me. Against the glass wall overlooking the escarpment, on the plush carpet in front of the fireplace, bent over the granite countertop…

"You smell so fucking good," Hudson whispers in my ear while Alana's back is turned. "Think we can get her to wait outside while we view the rest in private?"

Even as I shush him, heat pools low in my abdomen.

"Sorry, what was that?" Alana asks, turning toward us. She tilts her head as I scurry from Hudson. "Are you okay, Laura? Your face is all flushed. Wait, I know why."

My heart stops as she gives me a knowing nod.

"Hot flash, right? Menopause is such a bitch." She makes a commiserative cluck. "I'm not there yet, but my sister is, and she's your age."

*Your age.* Whether she meant the words critically or not, they hit me like a dart to a bullseye.

"Yes, just a bit overheated." I force an agreeable smile. "Think I'll step outside for a minute. You and Hudson go ahead and check out the rest of the house. I'll catch up."

"Sure thing." She points toward an archway. "That's a little home office I was going to show you next. There are

French doors to the back deck. You can go out there and cool off with the breeze."

"Thanks." I don't look back, but the weight of Hudson's stare lights up every cell in my body. Joining him for this viewing was a mistake. Any public togetherness will be, if we can't get our pheromones under control. Not that I want to control them. God, why would I, when the last eighteen hours have been the most exciting of my life?

I close my eyes and tip my head back as sweet summer air blows in from the lake below. Even without seeing the upstairs, I love this property. If he doesn't mind being mortgaged to the tits until he's a sexy silver fox, he should buy it. I would if I could.

"Beautiful view." The click of a door follows his deep voice.

I force myself not to look at him. To focus on the topic at hand instead. "It is. Whether it's calm or wild, Lake Erie is always beautiful." I point toward a dark arm in the distance. "That's Long Point. Definitely worth a daytrip sometime."

"Then we'll have to go. But I wasn't talking about the lake, I was referring to you." His breath tickles my cheek, he's standing so close behind me. "Everything okay?" he asks, sweeping my hair aside and cupping my bare shoulder with one warm, capable hand.

Electricity crackles between us as I meet his gaze. "You shouldn't be touching me like this."

"You're right." His eyes twinkle with that irresistible smolder. He moves closer, his solid body pressed against my back as he trails his fingers down my arm, grazing my breast in the process. "I should be doing a much more thorough job."

"Alana could be watching." My body cries at the loss when I shift sideways, putting an obvious space between us at the railing. "She can't see us like that. Everyone in town will know there's something going on between us if she sees us standing too close, or…touching."

# Fleshing It Out

"So what?"

I do my best to school my expression. The less emotion the nosey realtor sees on my face, the better. "Last night was incredible. And this morning. And as many other days and nights as you want to spend together in private. But, our hooking up can't become public knowledge."

"That's what you think we're doing—hooking up?" There's no smoothness in his voice now, just rough, hard edges on every word.

"I'm forty-five and you're thirty, what else could it be?"

"A relationship. The beginning of a great one."

The magnets are in full force, and I hold the railing to prevent myself from gravitating toward him. "It would be great—for a while—then it would end because I'm forty-five and you're thirty. And I'd be the middle-aged woman who fucked her hot tenant to get back at her ex for moving on with a younger woman. That's not the way I want my story to go. I told you before, I don't want to be known as the rebound cougar."

His jaw clenches, the mouth that looks so good when he smiles becoming a thin, straight line. "And I don't want to be your temporary, dirty little secret."

"Okay." I nod because…what else can I do? Leave, that's what. I walk away, giving him a wide berth as I head for the stairs at the side of the deck. I pause on the top step, and find him watching me when I look back. "It's a gorgeous property, and what I saw of the house is wonderful. Definitely worth considering, if my opinion still matters."

"It's always going to matter. I wish you believed that."

I believe he means it now, but I have to be realistic. Think about the future, and not get lost in this fantasy moment. "I have to go," I say, forcing a smile, and holding back tears until my back is turned on this perfect man I know isn't mine to keep.

# chapter six

. . .

## laura

YOU CAN WALK PRETTY MUCH ANYWHERE in Hope Harbor. After walking home from the real estate viewing, I quickly packed a duffel and took off. I've been promising and postponing a visit to my lifelong best friend's new cottage-country digs, and she was more than happy to get my, "Hey, is now a good time for a visit? Please?" message.

The time away didn't do much for my aching heart, but her company was nice. Well, aside from Beth's repeated, "God, you're a dumbass" comments. Her arguments that I should enjoy my relationship with Hudson while it lasts would be sound if we weren't talking about having it in Hope Harbor. It's a great town for many reasons, but the raging gossip mill isn't one of them.

Even with that, there's still a sense of homecoming when I reach the town's limits. Living alone, being self-employed, with the ability to work from anywhere, I could go anywhere. There's nowhere I'd rather be than Hope Harbor. I'll just have

Fleshing It Out

to figure out how to avoid Hudson as long as he lives here too.

Though, maybe that won't be long. He's young. It's early in his career. He could up and move at any point. Or, he may simply decide not to settle here after all. Real estate isn't plentiful, and I certainly didn't give him a reason to stay.

Honestly, I expect him to be gone already. From my house, for sure. I know he hated living out of a suitcase in a hotel room, but I doubt he'll want to share air with me after the things I said. I almost texted an apology this week. "Almost" being I typed out a message and hit Send, but it bounced back, undelivered. Five times. Beth blamed it on spotty internet service. I took it as a sign to let the man go.

My pulse kicks into overdrive when I turn onto my quiet street. His black car is in my driveway. He should be at the office on a Friday afternoon. Unless…

I accelerate, pulling in beside his car faster than necessary, and tapping a quick text to my son the moment I'm parked.

ME:
> Did Hudson quit working there?

"Come on, answer." When talking to my phone doesn't net me an immediate reply, I drill my fingers on the screen. Somehow, that accidentally sends Seth a string of random emojis—including an eggplant, a drooling face, and a red exclamation point. "Oh, shit."

SETH:
> Day drinking again, Mom? I thought you only did that with Aunt Beth.

His reply pops up, followed by several laughing-face emojis. My boy is so funny. And sweet. Twenty-five and still referring to my best friend as his aunt.

Karla Doyle

SETH:
No, he didn't quit. But he's not here, he took off in a hurry a while ago. Why?

Seth's second message appears, and my heart does a traitorous leap.

ME:
Just wondered. Put your phone away, you shouldn't be texting while you're on the clock.

SETH:
Says the woman who texted me a question during work hours.

Another laughing-face emoji follows, then a red heart. He's a good boy, that grownup kid of mine.

It's a relief Hudson didn't quit. Seth says they're overrun with jobs, and it's a great place to work. Hudson hasn't been there long enough to have vacation time. Maybe he's sick. A knot forms in my stomach, and I hurry into the house, ready and willing to switch into caregiver mode, if he'd even accept it from me.

There's music playing when I enter. Country music, coming from the back of the house. The kitchen and my office are the only possible sources, neither of which make sense if he stayed home sick.

The song changes as I enter the kitchen. *Let's Give Them Something to Talk About.* There's no way that's a coincidence, or that I'll be able to listen to it again without a lump in my throat. But that's on me—I'm the one who didn't want to give them something to talk about.

My pulse is a heavy drumbeat in my temples. My mouth is dry from holding my breath as I follow the music to its source—my office.

## Fleshing It Out

Hudson rises as I enter. As handsome as my brain wouldn't let me forget in the five days I've been away.

"You're not at work," I say, keeping a safe distance. Safe from myself, because I want nothing more than to cross the room and plaster myself against him. "Are you sick? Do you need anything?"

"Yeah, I need you."

I can't address his statement without losing my footing or coming across as a bitch, so I ignore it. Externally. Internally, I'll cling to the memory of those words for a long time to come. "I thought you might've moved out while I was away."

"You thought, or you hoped?"

"Thought," I say softly.

Hands in the pockets of his dark slacks, he closes the distance between us. "I'm not the kind of man who'd leave without an explanation."

My foolish heart sinks, but I catch it before it bottoms out. I'm an independent woman. A survivor. No man is going to take that from me. Not even one who ticks every box I've ever dreamed of. "You don't owe me an explanation. Our last conversation covered everything, I think."

"Not everything *I* wanted to say."

The knot in my stomach tightens because he's right. "It wasn't fair of me to take off without giving you the opportunity to tell me what you really think. You're welcome to do that now. I deserve it."

"You're right, you do deserve it."

I take a steadying breath, then nod. "Say what's on your mind. I can take it."

"I hope so," he says, moving closer.

He smells as good as I remember, and when he cups my face and tips it upward, everything that's happened since the ill-fated real estate viewing fades from existence.

"I came here looking for a temporary place to stay. The second I saw you, I knew it was going to be a hell of a lot more.

More than the physical chemistry. Every day, the connection gets stronger. You walk into the room, and I feel everything click into place. I've made some choices that weren't even choices. I just knew I had to make them, even if they seemed 'out there' at the time. Smaller click moments. Now, I know every one of those things happened to bring me here. To you. To us."

I'm so tempted to throw practicality to the wind and get swept away by this incredible man. But... "I can't." I cover his hands with mine and slide them from my face.

A sob threatens in my chest when he walks out without another word. I did it. We're done. I've gotten through to him, pushed him away for good.

White shirtsleeves rolled to mid-forearms, a manila folder in one hand, he strides back into the room. "A week ago, before we spent the night together, I asked you to look at that house with me. I didn't tell you everything though. I didn't tell you I'd already put a deposit down, to make sure nobody swooped in with an offer before we could."

"Before *we* could?" I semi-stagger backward, curling my fingers around the edge of the countertop for support. "Why would you do that? I can't do that."

"You say *can't* a lot," he says, his sexy smolder finding its home on his handsome face.

"You're right." I shake my head and smile, because *his* smile all it takes to render me happy, if only for this moment.

He sets the folder beside me and opens it to a form filled with text, then brackets me between his arms. "We bought the house."

"That's not possible. We can't. I can't."

"I hate to sound like your editor, but you need to use better words." He winks, and I'm powerless to do anything other than laugh until I sigh. "You think you're too old for me, but you're not. You think I'm going to get tired of you, but that's impossible."

## Fleshing It Out

"It's not. Fifteen years might seem inconsequential to you today, but with each year that goes by, that number will matter more."

"You're right, because every year we're together, I'm going to appreciate and value you more." Stroking my face, he looks so deeply in to my eyes, it makes my toes tingle. "Every day I get with you, I'm going to love you more."

*Love.* Did he just say—

"You needed time to think, so I waited. But every minute without you was empty. Wasted time we should've been together. I had to power off my phone so I wouldn't call you. I asked Seth where you were, and almost drove to Muskoka to tell you."

"To tell me we bought a house together without my knowledge, permission, or money?"

"No," he says, chuckling softly. "To tell you I'm in love with you."

"You're...in love with me?"

"Completely," he says, dipping his head to brush the words across my lips. "Real deal, all in, head over heels in love with you. We can sell the house tomorrow if you don't want it. Find something else, or stay right here. Hell, we can live in a box on the side of the road. I don't care where we are, as long as you're with me. On my proud fucking arm. Holding my hand. Wearing my ring, one day, when you're ready."

I might be crazy to follow my heart, but I'm crazy happy when I'm with him. A happiness unlike any other. Better than anything I've created for fictional people. Hudson's right—I deserve this happiness. I'd be crazy not to follow my heart. To grab on to him and never let him go.

"I love you too," I whisper. The admission is like pulling the pin on a floodgate of emotional truth. A sob wrenches free, and tears blur my view of his handsome face. "I just realized that I haven't said those words and meant them in such a long time."

"Do you mean them now?"

"Yes. God, yes." There's no stopping the waterworks once they start, so I let the tears fall as I bury my face against his chest. "I'm sorry. We should be making out right now, halfway to the bedroom, and instead, I'm crying, probably ruining your shirt."

He wraps me in a perfect hug, his chuckle vibrating beneath my ear. "Ruin away, sweetheart. You know I don't like wearing shirts."

"Understatement of the year," I say, laughing until there are no more tears. I take a deep breath and smile up at him, my arms twined behind his neck. "Take me to bed and show me how much you love me."

"Hope you don't have plans, because that's going to require a lot of time." Grinning, he scoops me off my feet, and heads for the stairs.

"How about the rest of my life? Is that enough?"

"That's perfect, sweetheart."

And it is. It really is.

# epilogue

...

## hudson

I LIKE to do things up big. Laura says it's in my genes. She's partly right, but my love of big gestures, my need to make them, has more to do with her than my Greek heritage.

Laying the verbal smackdown on her ex during our first date at The Undertow. Putting her name on the deed of our house before we'd worked through our shit. Some people would say I go too far. Laura's never said that, though. She shakes her head sometimes, but I know she loves my big gestures. That's why she's getting another one tonight.

Standing in the foyer of the house we've called home since moving in last month, I flick my wrist to check my watch. We're not running late, we're ahead of schedule. I just want to get there. To the restaurant. The moment. The next step in our life together.

"Wow, you look hot."

I turn at the sound of her voice, my dick growing instantly hard at the sight of my lady coming down the stairs. "And you look fucking sexy as hell. If we didn't have a reservation, I'd turn you around and take you back to bed right now."

"We could change our reservation, I'm sure we can find *something* to snack on until later." She breathes the words against my neck as she kisses it. Then she's on her knees in front of me, licking her lips as she unzips my pants and takes my dick out.

I'm the one standing, towering over her, but I'm powerless. Every cell in my body is on fire as I watch my dick disappear between her ruby lips. "Your mouth is amazing." I thread my fingers through her hair, messing it up because I'm an animal. Her beast. I know that's how she wants it. "You know what it does to me, having you on your knees."

*"Mmmhmm…"* Her hum vibrates around my dick.

I groan at the hard suction. But it's the slack in her jaw that follows that makes my inner beast roar. I know what she wants. "You need me to fuck your mouth, baby? To come down your throat and watch you swallow every drop?"

She moans around my cock, nodding, blinking her beautiful eyes. So fucking sexy. Her dress is too tight to maneuver, so she presses her fingers against the front, rubbing the fabric. I'll take care of that for her. With pleasure.

I curl my fingers into a fist, use my grip on her hair to guide her mouth up and down my dick. Faster, harder, until heat rages at the base of my cock. "Fuck, baby, fuck…" I groan, unloading deep in her throat. Man of my word, I hold her there until I feel her swallow.

Her eyes are glassy as I guide her to her feet. Then to the stairs. She pulls her bottom lip between her teeth when I tug her dress up to her waist. Gasps when I rip the thin strings of her panties, then stuff the scrap in my pocket.

"My turn," I say, positioning her on the fifth stair with her thighs spread wide. Doesn't matter that I just came. That I ate her pussy and fucked her before getting ready to go out. The second I taste her, my dick's at attention. I'm never going to get enough of her.

Fleshing It Out

She arches as I bury my face between her legs. Pushes her fingers through my hair, tugs me closer, holds me in place as she grinds against my tongue.

As if I'd want to be anywhere else.

She's close within seconds. Coming undone beneath me way too soon.

I take her down, gentling my contact, but not letting her go when she slides her hands to my shoulders. "That wasn't enough for me, sweetheart. We need to work on your hair trigger."

She pushes me away playfully, her laughter fucking lighting up my world.

I take her hands and pull her up with me. "Let's go, gorgeous. There's a bottle of wine and a hell of a view waiting for us."

She raises an eyebrow at me while attempting to smooth her sexed-up hair. "Are you sure we can make it?"

"Been positive of that since the moment we met," I say, wrapping my arms around her from behind. "Are you?"

"Very much so."

"You're getting much better with your word choices."

"Gee, thanks." She shakes her head, yipping when I smack her sexy ass.

Threading our fingers together, I motion at the door. "Let's go celebrate."

She's glowing as we head out for what she believes is a celebration of her latest release. Something I recently discovered she's always wanted to do, but nobody has ever stepped up to make happen.

I'm the man to step up. For this and everything else. For the rest of our lives.

## laura

A Tuesday in September shouldn't require a reservation at The Undertow, but Hudson insisted we make one anyway. He likes to make a big deal of me. It's pointless to tell him it's unnecessary. Besides, I love it. "Good for you, when do you get paid for it?" and "Way to go, Mom" sums up the enthusiasm I received for the first forty-nine books I published.

Hudson doesn't care if I earn a dollar a month or ten thousand. Not only because he's got a Greek inheritance in the bank, though that certainly takes the pressure off. He's impressed by my stories, proud of my achievements. When he found out this release is my fiftieth, he insisted we celebrate it properly. Date night was his idea.

Adding the appetizer at home was mine. Losing my panties in the process was extra spice I didn't plan for. I've never gone commando in public. Like everything else with Hudson, it's exciting and safe at the same time.

At the top of the steps, I let go of his hand, slide my arms around his waist, and snuggle into his side. I'm getting better at public displays of affection with him.

"I love this." The smile on his face makes any judgmental stares we might get worthwhile.

"I love you." I've gotten a lot better at saying that, too.

He kisses my temple, the smile on his face becoming a full-width grin as we turn into the dining area. "Happy release day."

"Oh my God."

There's a "Congratulations" banner across the hostess's desk with my book cover and my names—both of them. That explains the multiple conversations we've had recently about my pseudonym. Why I chose to use one, and whether I care if anyone around town knows it's me. It's safe to say *he's* not embarrassed by my work.

Fleshing It Out

"I can't believe you did tha..." The rest of my words vanish with what I'm sure is a gape-mouthed stare at the hostess, who's wearing a t-shirt with my new release's cover screen-printed on the front.

Apparently, Hudson did more than ask them to hang a banner.

"Congratulations! I didn't know Hope Harbor had a famous author until your husband came in to plan this awesome party, but I bought and read two of your books already. From the cowboy series. They're great! Do you have a favorite of your books? Oh, I read those cowboy ones on my e-reader, but do you sell autographed copies?"

It takes a few seconds for my brain to catch up. I've never been publicly acknowledged as an author in real life, and now, all of this. "Wow, thank you. Um, no, I don't have one favorite, but there are a few that I love a bit more than the others, and yes, you can order personalized copies on my website. But if you tell me which book you're interested in, I'd be happy to drop one off next time you're working."

"Really? Thank you!" She makes a *squeeing* sound, then gathers some menus and motions for us to follow her. "Your table is ready and waiting."

Hudson lets the hostess get a few paces ahead. "My *wife* is famous," he says, leaning down to speak near my ear.

Heat rises to my cheeks. "I'm sorry I didn't correct her. I will when we get to the table."

"I wasn't complaining, sweetheart."

I'm spared from discussing our inaccurate marital status when multiple servers wearing the same custom-printed t-shirt as the hostess come into view. "Oh my God. How many shirts did you have made?"

"Enough for everyone working tonight."

I meet his gaze while taking the chair he pulls out. "How much did you pay them?"

"I didn't. Sometimes you just have to ask and yes is the answer." God, he looks smug. Handsome and sexy, but definitely smug.

"There's more coming, isn't there?"

"There's *always* more coming."

I shake my head, letting the innuendo slide.

We make it through a champagne toast, appetizers, and dinner without the *more* I suspected materializing. It was only playful teasing, and that's kind of a relief. I'm not accustomed to being the center of attention.

After our table is cleared, I reach across to stroke his rugged jaw with its sexy five o'clock shadow. "Thank you for tonight. The fuss was silly and wonderful, and I appreciate it so much. You made this an incredibly special evening I'll always remember."

"I hope so." He kisses my hand, smiling as our server arrives with a tray and unloads two desserts we didn't order.

"Enjoy your peachy queen cobblers."

Not for the first time, and certainly not for the last, I laugh loud enough to turn heads. "Sorry," I say, pulling my lips between my teeth to stifle further noise. I wait for the confused waitress to leave before laughing again. "*Peachy queen* cobbler? Really? They don't even make peach cobbler here."

"Like I said before, sometimes you just have to ask and hope the answer is yes." He pushes his chair back and rises, then moves to my side of the table, where he goes down to one knee.

"What are you doing?" I whisper, my heart galloping in my chest.

"Asking. Hoping for a yes." He takes a velvet box from his pocket and opens it, revealing the world's most perfect diamond ring. "I love you more than any words can say, but I'm giving it a shot because I'm learning from the best. Laura,

Fleshing It Out

you're my home. My happily ever after. I want to spend the rest of my life making your wishes and fantasies come true. Will you marry me?"

"Yes. Oh my God, yes," I say, throwing myself at him as the room erupts with clapping and hooting. The perfect ending to a storybook evening. The perfect beginning to the next chapter of our fairytale romance.

Are you ready to go back to Hope Harbor for another steamy, feel-good love story? All books in the Hope Harbor series are standalone romances, and can be read in any order.

**Dad Bod Wingman**
**Heart Beats**
**Last Call Casanova**
**Doggy Style**
**The Deal With Love**
**Resorting to Love**
**King of Her Dreams**
**12 Days**

More Hope Harbor romances are on deck!

Karla Doyle

## get karla's newsletter

Join Karla's mailing list and stay updated on new releases, sales, freebies, and more!

www.karladoyle.com/newsletter

# also by karla doyle

Wedded Miss

Dad Bod Wingman (Hope Harbor series)

Last Call Casanova (Hope Harbor series)

Fleshing It Out (Hope Harbor series)

The Deal With Love (Hope Harbor series)

Doggy Style (Hope Harbor series)

Resorting to Love (linked to Hope Harbor series)

Heart Beats (Hope Harbor series)

King of Her Dreams (Hope Harbor series)

Puck That

White Lie Christmas (linked to Hope Harbor series)

Dating the Doubter

Heart of Texas

Now You See Me (a monster-lite romance)

The Beast Within (a monster romance)

Gingerbread Man (Man of the Month Club)

12 Days (Hope Harbor series)

Gift Wrapped

Cup of Sugar (Close to Home—Book 1)

Icing on the Cake (Close to Home—Book 2)

Sweet as Candy (Close to Home—Book 3)

Body of Work (Very Personal Training—Book 1)

Worth the Wait (Very Personal Training—Book 2)

Game Plan

More Than Words

Crossing the Line

**For the most up-to-date list of Karla's books, visit her website www.karladoyle.com**

# about the author

A small-town girl with some big-city experience, Karla resides in Southwestern Ontario with her husband and two all-grown-up kids. She studied fashion design in college and spent 20+ years working in that industry before succumbing to the writing muse. When she's not writing the sexy stories that swirl around in her head, you can find her reading a romance while cuddling her adorable pets.

Karla loves hearing from readers! Connect with her online, or send her an email: karla@karladoyle.com.

Join Karla's mailing list to stay up to date on all her news.
**www.karladoyle.com/newsletter**

Made in the USA
Columbia, SC
20 April 2023